# Dear Parent:

Congratulations! Your child is taking the first steps on an exciting journey. The destination? Independent reading!

**STEP INTO READING**® will help your child get there. The program offers five steps to reading success. Each step includes fun stories and colorful art. There are also Step into Reading Sticker Books, Step into Reading Math Readers, Step into Reading Phonics Readers, Step into Reading Write-In Readers, and Step into Reading Phonics Boxed Sets—a complete literacy program with something to interest every child.

## Learning to Read, Step by Step!

**Ready to Read   Preschool–Kindergarten**
• big type and easy words • rhyme and rhythm • picture clues
For children who know the alphabet and are eager to begin reading.

**Reading with Help   Preschool–Grade 1**
• basic vocabulary • short sentences • simple stories
For children who recognize familiar words and sound out new words with help.

**Reading on Your Own   Grades 1–3**
• engaging characters • easy-to-follow plots • popular topics
For children who are ready to read on their own.

**Reading Paragraphs   Grades 2–3**
• challenging vocabulary • short paragraphs • exciting stories
For newly independent readers who read simple sentences with confidence.

**Ready for Chapters   Grades 2–4**
• chapters • longer paragraphs • full-color art
For children who want to take the plunge into chapter books but still like colorful pictures.

**STEP INTO READING**® is designed to give every child a successful reading experience. The grade levels are only guides. Children can progress through the steps at their own speed, developing confidence in their reading, no matter what their grade.

Remember, a lifetime love of reading starts with a single step!

Special thanks to Vicki Jaeger, Monica Okazaki, Ann McNeill, Emily Kelly, Sharon Woloszyk, Julia Phelps, Tanya Mann, Rob Hudnut, David Wiebe, Shelley Dvi-Vardhana, Michelle Cogan, Rainmaker Entertainment, Walter P. Martishius, Carla Alford, Rita Lichtwardt, Kathy Berry, and Miranda Nolte

Published in the United States by Random House Children's Books, a division of Random House, Inc., 1745 Broadway, New York, NY 10019, and in Canada by Random House of Canada Limited, Toronto.

Visit us on the Web!
StepIntoReading.com
www.randomhouse.com/kids
www.barbie.com

Educators and librarians, for a variety of teaching tools, visit us at
www.randomhouse.com/teachers

ISBN: 978-0-375-86931-0 (trade) — ISBN: 978-0-375-96931-7 (lib. bdg.)
Printed in the United States of America   10 9 8 7 6 5 4 3 2 1

## Barbie™ PRINCESS Charm SCHOOL

Adapted by Ruth Homberg

Based on the screenplay by Elise Allen

Illustrated by Ulkutay Design Group

Random House 🏠 New York

Blair lives
with her mom
and her sister, Emily.

One day,
Blair wins a spot
in Princess Charm School!
Emily is very happy
for Blair.

Blair goes
to the school.
It is in Gardania.
She meets a dog
named Prince.

Blair also meets Madame Privet, Hadley, and Isla. Each girl gets a uniform and her own sprite!

Dame Devin wants
her daughter, Delancy,
to be Princess
of Gardania.

Hadley says
the real princess
was lost.

Dame Devin and Delancy
do not want Blair
to be a princess.

Blair works hard.

She learns to walk
like a princess.

One day,

Delancy trips her!

Blair goes
to dance class.
She dances
with Prince Nicholas.

Prince Nicholas
likes Blair.
Delancy is mad.

All the girls
get ready
for a tea party.

They take baths.
Their sprites paint
their nails.

Blair, Hadley, and Isla
go back to their room.
Someone has torn
their clothes!

But the girls make
new outfits.
They go
to the tea party.

The girls see
a painting
of young Queen Isabella.
She looks like Blair!

Delancy sees the picture, too.

Is Blair the lost Princess of Gardania?

After the party,
Dame Devin hides
a necklace
under Blair's pillow.

Blair gets in trouble.

Dame Devin says

Blair stole the necklace!

Delancy thinks Blair
is the lost princess.
She helps Blair find
Gardania's magic crown.
When the true princess
wears the crown,
it glows.

The three friends sneak
into the palace.

The girls
find the crown!
Blair reaches
for it.

But Dame Devin
stops her!

Dame Devin locks
the girls up.
They work as a team.
Hadley opens
the vault's keypad.
Blair connects her phone.
Isla sings the secret code.

The door opens!
The girls escape.

Dame Devin tries
to crown Delancy
Princess of Gardania.

Blair runs
into the ballroom
just in time.
Dame Devin is angry!

The sprites put
the magic crown
on Blair's head.

The crown glows.
Blair is the lost
Princess of Gardania!

Blair thanks
her friends.
Emily and her mom move
into the palace.
They live happily
ever after!